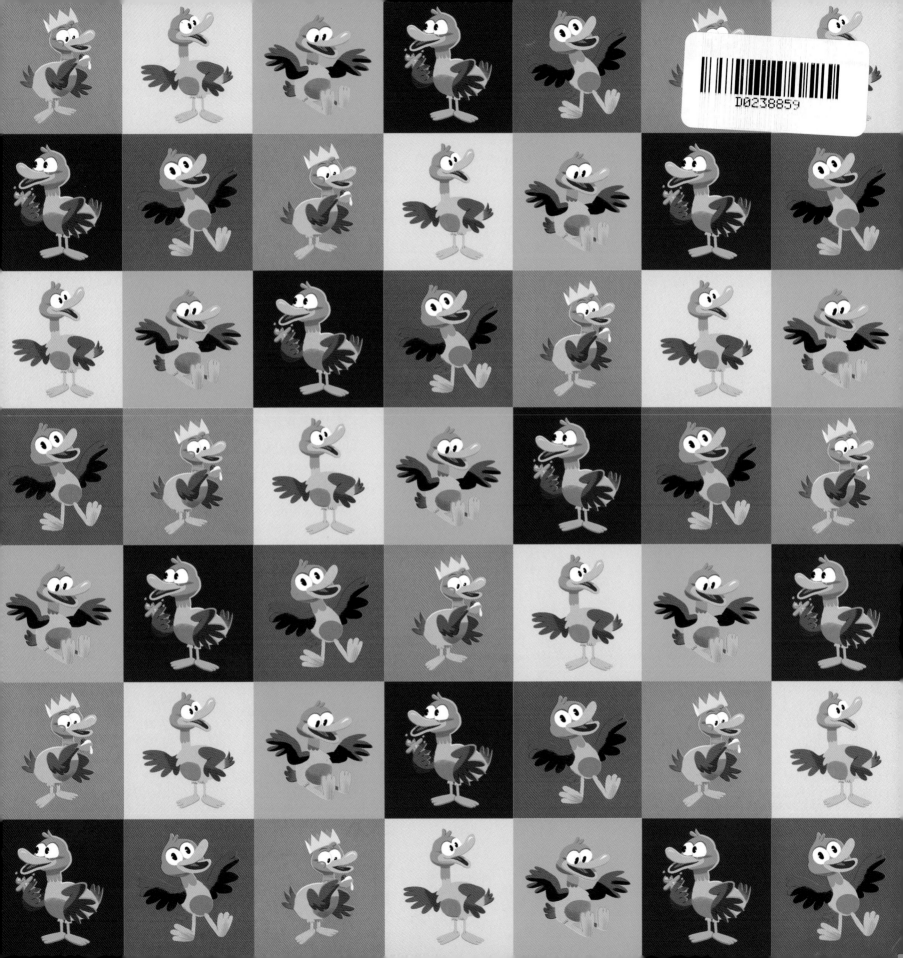

IMAGINE THAT

Licensed exclusively to Imagine That Publishing Ltd
Tide Mill Way, Woodbridge, Suffolk, IP12 1AP, UK
www.imaginethat.com
Copyright © 2021 Imagine That Group Ltd
All rights reserved
2 4 6 8 9 7 5 3 1
Manufactured in China

Written by Sam Samson
Illustrated by Erin Hunting

ISBN 978-1-80105-174-3

A catalogue record for this book is available from the British Library

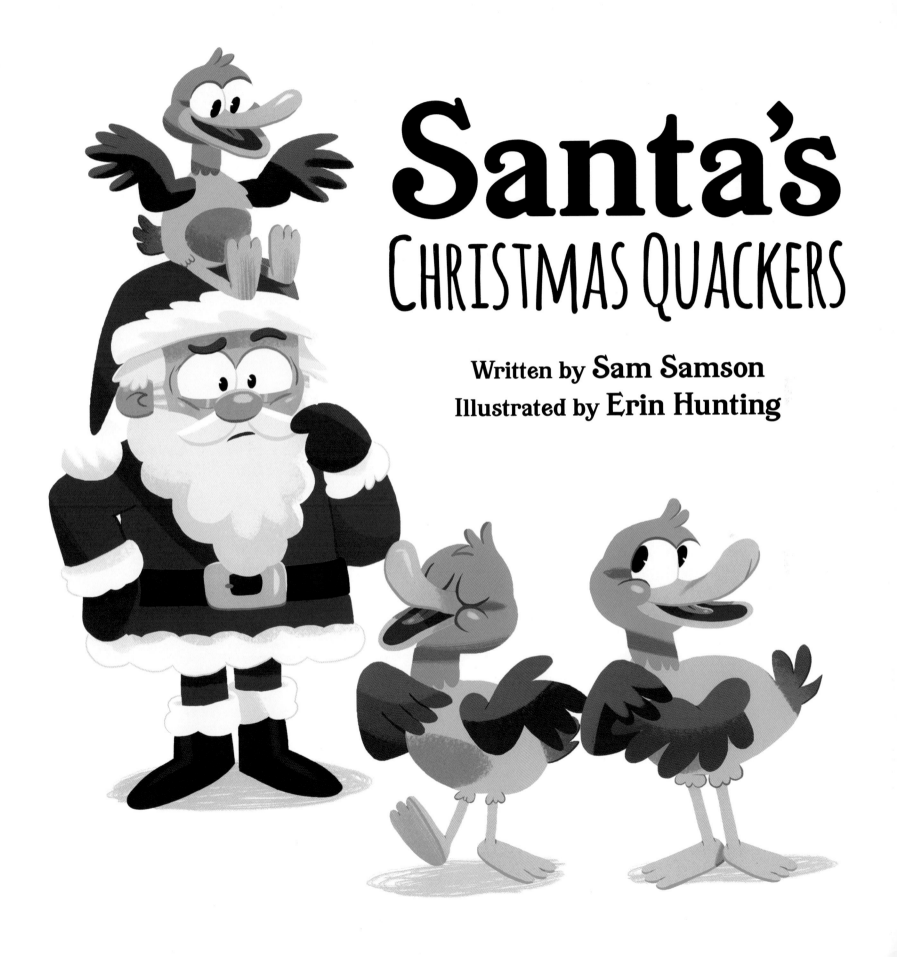

Santa's
CHRISTMAS QUACKERS

Written by **Sam Samson**

Illustrated by **Erin Hunting**

It was that time of year ... time for Santa's elves to choose the Christmas crackers. This year it was Holly and Ivy's turn.

'Let's have these!' said Holly. 'They are the very best crackers!' The crackers were full of party hats, gifts and jokes.

The next day, a big delivery of boxes arrived. Santa and the elves looked at the boxes standing in the snow.

They were jiggling and joggling ... and making the strangest sounds!

Carefully, the elves peeled back the lids to peep inside.
They spied a beady eye here, a shiny feather there ...
and quacky beaks **EVERYWHERE!**

'These are not the very best Christmas crackers!' cried Santa, looking at Holly and Ivy. 'You must have ordered Christmas Quackers by mistake. We must send them back at once!'

North Pole

'But aren't we what you ordered?'
asked one Christmas Quacker.
'We are *very* good at jokes!'

'And they are much funnier than cracker jokes,' said another Christmas Quacker. 'Please keep us!'

Santa groaned.

The elves groaned.

What could Santa do? He had *no* Christmas crackers, and *lots* of joke-telling Christmas Quackers instead. And every joke was bad!

But it was Christmas – the time for fun and kindness. Santa had a plan! The elves would make Christmas crackers, and the Christmas Quackers could stay and help! But they must practise writing *good* jokes.

After lots of practice, the Christmas Quackers were ready.
They joined the elves in the packing room
and started to write new jokes.

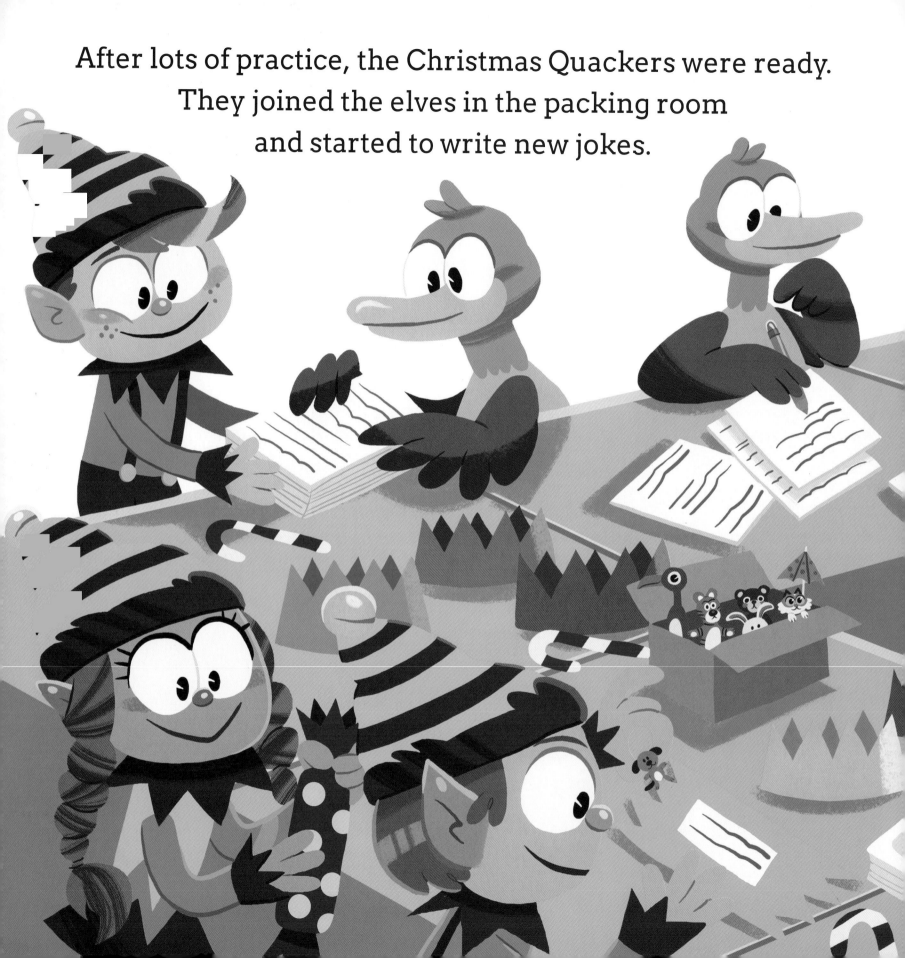

Santa named the cracker collection 'Christmas Quackers', after his feathered helpers.

Everyone worked very hard to get ready for Christmas. On Christmas Eve, Santa did his big delivery, then it was time to relax and enjoy a huge Christmas feast.

Holly picked up one of the new crackers and handed it to Santa. 'Pull!' she cried.

'Where does Santa go when he's ill?' asked Holly.

'To the Elf Centre!' sighed Santa.

'*NOOOOOOOOO!*' shouted all the elves, giggling.

Perhaps the Christmas Quackers would need
a tiny bit of extra practice before next Christmas!